SWORD GIRL

TOURNAMENT TROUBLE

FRANCES WATTS

ILLUSTRATED BY GREGORY ROGERS

ALLEN&UNWIN
SYDNEY•MELBOURNE•AUCKLAND•LONDON

Allen & Unwin
83 Alexander Street
Crows Nest NSW 2065
Australia
Phone: (61 2) 8425 0100
Fax: (61 2) 9906 2218
Email: info@allenandunwin.com
Web: www.allenandunwin.com

A Cataloguing-in-Publication entry is available from the National Library
of Australia
www.trove.nla.gov.au

ISBN 978 1 74237 989 0

Cover design by Seymour Designs
Cover illustration by Gregory Rogers
Text design by Seymour Designs
Set in 16/21 pt Adobe Jenson Pro by Seymour Designs
5 ☒☒☒ PP☒☒ ☒ ☒☒ S☒☒☒☒☒☒☒☒☒☒ C☒S☒☒☒☒ ☒☒☒ S☒G☒☒ S☒T☒
☒☒☒■ SP T☒, ☒☒ D3. P☒☒☒☒☒☒C ☒ S☒☒ P☒☒☒☒☒ ☒☒☒☒☒ ☒ D☒☒☒

10 9 8 7 6 5 4

For Lady Christa the Best (friend)
F. W.

For Matt
G. R.

CHAPTER 1

'FLAMANT FOR VICTORY!'

The battle cry was so loud it carried through the thick stone walls of the armoury and all the way to the sword chamber where Tommy was working.

'Flamant for victory!'

The cry was echoed by dozens of voices, followed by the thunder of horses' hooves across the great courtyard of Flamant

Castle. The castle's squires were practising their jousting skills in preparation for the tournament that was only five days away.

Tommy held up the sword she was polishing and saw the blade gleam in the flickering light of the candle on the wall. With a sigh, she replaced it in the rack then picked up another sword from the pile on the floor beside her and dipped her rag into the pot of clove-scented oil.

The squires, who were training to be knights, would be jousting with lances on horseback, but the knights themselves would be competing in sword fights. The knights had been practising every day, and Tommy had been polishing and sharpening their swords from morning till night. In all the months she had been

Keeper of the Blades, she had never been so busy.

The cries of the squires were drowned out by a clatter as Reynard, the Keeper of the Bows, burst into the armoury and dropped an armful of shields on the smith's wooden table.

'You've been gone a while,' the smith observed with a grunt. 'Busy in town, is it?'

'You should see it, Smith,' Reynard replied. 'All the houses have banners on them in the colours of Flamant Castle, and the town is full of merchants who've come from all over for the fair in Jonglers Field.'

Tommy, who had lifted her head from her work to listen, ducked it again when she saw Reynard glance in her direction. Reynard had hated Tommy ever since she

had been made the Keeper of the Blades instead of him.

But Reynard must have seen that Tommy was listening for he raised his voice to say, 'There are going to be dancers and musicians – I even saw some acrobats practising their tumbling. I feel sorry for anyone who's missing all the fun.'

Reynard didn't sound very sorry at all, Tommy thought, as she scrubbed furiously at a smudge of dirt on the blade of a sword. She had been so excited when Sir Walter the Bald announced that Flamant Castle would be holding a tournament, and all the knights and squires of neighbouring Roses Castle had been invited. There was to be a grand procession followed by three days of competitions, with a big feast held every night. And on top of that, there was to be a fair in Jonglers Field, with stalls and games and entertainment. Tommy longed to see the preparations, but whenever Smith needed an errand run to the blacksmith in town, he sent Reynard instead of her. 'I'm sorry, Sword Girl,' he would say, 'but you're needed here.'

Tommy sighed again.

'What's the matter, dearie?'

The voice came from a sabre behind her. It was Nursie, one of the Old Wrecks. When Tommy had first become Keeper of the Blades, responsible for looking after all the bladed weapons of Flamant Castle, the Old Wrecks had been neglected for years. But Tommy soon discovered that the swords in the small rack in the darkest corner of the sword chamber were inhabited by the spirits of their previous owners.

'I'm just thinking about the tournament,' Tommy told her.

'Ooh, the tournament,' said Nursie. 'What an exciting time. Why, I remember

when my little darling fought in his first tournament. He won, of course.' Nursie's 'little darling', Tommy knew, was Sir Walter himself; Nursie had been his nursemaid.

A long-handled dagger with a deep voice chimed in, 'And don't forget the fair. All those stalls … There'll be leather goods and delicious pies and spices and candles and – oh, anything you can imagine. It's a fine time to be a merchant. Will you be buying anything at the fair, Sword Girl?'

'You merchants are all the same, Bevan Brumm,' Nursie scolded. 'Always wanting people to buy things. But our sword girl is more interested in the tournament, aren't you, dearie?'

While the sabre and the dagger

argued over which was better, a tournament or a fair, Tommy's spirits sank lower. She'd never seen a tournament *or* a fair.

As she sighed for a third time, a slender sword with a slightly curved blade spoke up. 'It must be hard to be cooped up here in the sword chamber when there's so much excitement going on outside.' Jasper Swann, a squire, had been close to Tommy's own age when he died. Perhaps that was why he often seemed to understand what she was feeling.

Tommy looked at the sword in her hand. 'I wish I could be out there in the courtyard,' she said. 'Riding a horse and jousting.' She thrust the sword forward at an imaginary opponent. It was Tommy's dearest wish to one day become a squire. 'But they'll probably never let a girl ride in a tournament,' she finished gloomily.

'Don't be downhearted, dearie,' Nursie advised. 'Your turn will come.'

'That's right, Sword Girl,' Jasper agreed. 'After all, whoever thought a kitchen girl would become the castle's Keeper of the Blades? And look how quickly you—'

But before he could finish they heard a cry so loud it made Tommy drop her sword in fright. 'What was that?' she gasped.

CHAPTER 2

TOMMY RUSHED TO THE DOOR of the armoury. Smith and Reynard were there already, watching the scene unfolding in the great courtyard. The squires had gathered around a boy who was lying on the flagstones. His face was pale and his eyes were closed.

'That's young Edward,' said Smith as Tommy joined them. 'He was Keeper of the Blades before you, Sword Girl.' He shook his head. 'Fell from his horse, poor lad.'

Sir Hugh, who had been leading the squires in their practice, was kneeling beside the injured boy.

'Go fetch the physician,' he ordered, his voice loud.

Edward moaned and Tommy felt a twinge of sympathy.

'There now, that's enough goggle-eyein',' said Smith as the physician hurried across the courtyard, his robes flapping. 'Back to work.'

Tommy returned to the sword chamber, still thinking of the pale-faced boy and his terrible cry. She hoped he would be all right.

When she had finally finished sharpening and polishing all the swords, Tommy hurried outside to find Lil. She would know if there was news about Edward. But Lil wasn't in any of her usual spots in the great courtyard – probably all the clamour and clatter of the knights and squires practising had disturbed her. So Tommy went through the low arch leading from the courtyard and out the castle gate. Sure enough, there was the black and white cat, lying on a patch of sun-warmed grass beside the moat. The crocodiddle, who guarded the moat, had his head resting on the bank beside her.

'Have you heard anything about Edward,

the squire who was thrown from his horse?' Tommy asked as she joined her friends. Tommy had discovered that most of the animals at Flamant Castle could talk, though they didn't talk to everyone – only to those who were good at listening, as Sir Benedict put it.

'Horses,' snorted the crocodiddle. 'The way people go on, you'd think the horse was

the only noble creature the castle had ever seen. And it's worse during tournaments. The horses get all dressed up in coats and hoods and wear ribbons in their tails. What about the noble crocodiddle? No one bothers with him.' He pouted and splashed the water with his tail.

Lil stretched then sat up. 'Edward is still being tended to by the physician, Tommy.'

'I hope he'll be able to ride in the tournament,' Tommy said. 'Think how disappointing it would be to miss out. I wish *I* was riding in the tournament.'

'Ah, but tournaments are not just for fun, you know,' said the cat. 'They're a good opportunity for knights and squires to practise their skills so they're ready for battle. And you have a big responsibility,

Tommy. Our knights need their swords to be in top condition if they are to perform well in the tournament. They are depending on their Keeper of the Blades.'

'You're right,' said Tommy, feeling guilty when she recalled her earlier grumbling in the sword chamber.

'What about me?' said the crocodiddle. 'Are they depending on me too?'

'Of course they are,' said the cat. 'We all depend on you all the time.'

The crocodiddle grinned, showing two enormous rows of teeth.

Tommy stood up. 'I'd better have some dinner and go to bed,' she said. 'I've got a lot of important work to do tomorrow.'

The next morning, as she crossed the courtyard on her way to the armoury, Tommy saw the small round figure of the physician staring into the sky.

'Pigeon ... Oh, Pigeon ...' he was calling. At first nothing happened, then there was a flutter of grey feathers and a cross voice said, 'I gave you some droppings the day before yesterday. How can you have run out already?' The carrier pigeon came to rest on a low wall.

'There's been an accident,' the physician explained. 'One of the squires fell during practice yesterday afternoon and he's badly hurt. I need some more droppings to make the cure.'

'How is Edward?' Tommy asked.

The physician looked grave. 'Broken leg,' he said. 'I doubt he'll be riding a horse again anytime soon.'

A broken leg? So poor Edward would have to miss out on the tournament after all, Tommy thought as she entered the armoury.

As usual, the air in the armoury was warm from the fire of the forge and the stones echoed with the clanging of a hammer striking metal.

'I just saw the physician,' Tommy reported when the smith paused in his work. 'Edward has broken his leg.'

'So, Flamant Castle will be one squire short for the tournament, eh?' the smith observed. 'Sir Walter won't like that.'

'Quite right,' said a voice behind them, making Tommy jump.

'Sir Benedict,' she said.

'Good morning, Tommy,' said the knight. 'Morning, Smith.'

The smith put down his hammer. 'Is it your shield again, Sir Benedict?' he asked.

'I'm afraid so,' said Sir Benedict. 'The strap has broken.'

The smith took the shield Sir Benedict held out and inspected it. 'If you didn't sling it around so much, you wouldn't have so many broken straps,' he told the knight.

If Flamant Castle's bravest knight minded the smith telling him how to fight, he didn't show it. He smiled and said, 'You're probably right, Smith. But can you fix it?'

The smith squinted at the strap then said, 'I s'pose I could do a quick fix with tacks, but you'll have to leave it with me – I've got all these other shields to see to first.'

'Of course,' said Sir Benedict. 'And how about you, Tommy? Are we keeping you busy too?'

'Yes, sir,' said Tommy. She led him into the sword chamber and showed him the pile of swords waiting for her attention. The pile seemed to have doubled in size overnight. 'But I don't mind.'

'Good girl. But I've got another job for you, Tommy. As you just heard, Edward's accident has left us one squire short for the tournament. What do you say?'

Tommy wasn't sure she'd understood. 'Do you mean … me?' she asked.

Sir Benedict nodded. 'That's right. I want *you* to fight in the tournament.'

CHAPTER 3

Tommy stared at the knight in amazement. 'Me?' she repeated. 'In the tournament?'

Sir Benedict nodded again. 'Would you like that?'

'Yes!' exclaimed Tommy. 'I mean, yes please, sir.' For a moment she just beamed at him, so full of excitement she was unable to speak. Then something occurred to her.

'But Sir Benedict, I've never ridden a horse before,' she confessed.

Sir Benedict frowned. 'Ah,' he said. 'I hadn't thought of that. I'm sorry, Tommy. It looks like I'll have to find someone else.'

Tommy's heart sank like a stone as he turned away.

'She can learn,' said a voice behind them.

Sir Benedict turned around. 'What was that, Jasper?' he asked.

'I said Sword Girl can learn, sir,' Jasper Swann repeated. 'She's as quick as anything.'

'It's true,' Nursie broke in. 'I've never seen anyone pick up new skills like our sword girl. She'll learn to ride a horse in no time.'

'Is that right?' said Sir Benedict.

'They are not wrong,' said Bevan Brumm in his dignified manner.

'Of course we're not wrong,' snapped Nursie. 'Now, what do you say, Sir Benedict: will you give our sword girl a chance?'

Tommy's heart pounded as Sir Benedict gazed at her thoughtfully.

'Yes,' he said at last. 'I will. Tommy, I'll ask the stable master to lend you one of my own mounts. Go to the stables tomorrow morning straight after breakfast. You can practise riding in the mornings and then join the other squires for jousting practice with Sir Hugh in the afternoons. You've got a lot to learn, and only three days to learn it in.'

'But what about all these swords?' Tommy asked, pointing to the pile.

'Don't worry about that.' Sir Benedict stepped out into the armoury. 'Smith, I've asked Tommy to take Edward's place in the tournament. She'll be doing a lot of practising in the next few days. Can you see to it that she has help with the work in the sword chamber?'

'That'll be no problem, Sir Benedict,' the smith assured him. Then his face split in a huge grin. 'Our sword girl fighting in the tournament, eh?'

As Sir Benedict left the armoury the smith shouted, 'Oi, Reynard!'

'What?' Reynard asked rudely from the bow chamber.

'Sword Girl needs to practise for the tournament. You'll have to help out looking after the blades.'

'What do you mean she's practising for the tournament?' the Keeper of the Bows demanded. He appeared in the doorway of the bow chamber, face set in a scowl.

Smith shrugged. 'Just what I said, lad. Sir Benedict has asked her to be in the tournament.'

Reynard's face turned as red as his hair. '*Her?*' he spluttered. 'In the tournament? And you want *me* to do her work?'

'No time like the present,' said Smith. 'There's a stack of swords that need cleaning. You can get started straight away. Sword Girl, I need some more of these small tacks to fix Sir Benedict's shield. Would you go to the blacksmith in town for me?'

'In town?' said Tommy, remembering Reynard's tales of the preparations going on for the fair. 'Yes please!'

She raced out of the armoury so fast she

almost
collided with
Sir Benedict, who
was standing outside
talking to Sir Hugh.

'Where are you off to in such a rush,
Tommy?' he asked.

'I'm going to town, sir,' she said. 'On an
errand for Smith.'

'Hmm, that reminds me … While you're
there, Tommy, perhaps you'd call by the

cloth merchant and ask him to have two lengths of pink cloth and one of sky blue sent to the castle.'

'Yes, Sir Benedict.'

As she ran across the flagstones towards the castle gate, Tommy had never been so happy. She was going to be in the tournament! She was going to learn to ride a horse! And best of all, she was closer than ever to her dream of being the first-ever girl squire!

CHAPTER 4

Tommy hurried along the road that led to the town gate. On one side of the road was the field where the tournament was to be held. Colourful tents were being erected and carpenters were building wooden platforms where the spectators would sit. Tommy could hardly believe that in only a few days' time she would be part of the procession of knights and squires making their way from the castle to the field. Her heart gave a nervous lurch at the thought that everyone from the castle and the town would be watching.

She turned to look at Jonglers Field on the other side of the road. Apart from a few travellers camped around the edge, the field was still deserted. It was hard to imagine it filled with all the colour and life of a fair.

But as she passed through the town gate Tommy decided it wasn't that hard to imagine after all, for the town was alive with activity. Outside the bakery she saw a small crowd had stopped to watch a man juggling loaves of bread. He was crying, 'Ouch, ouch, ouch,' as if they were too hot to hold. Tommy laughed along with the others then continued on her way.

There seemed to be about five times more people than usual crammed into the narrow street that led to the market square. Many of them were wheeling carts or carrying sacks, and quite a few of them were wearing strange clothes. The strangest of all were the four men standing still in the midst of the bustling crowd. Their clothes were patterned with bright stripes, and ribbons hung from their wrists. They were looking around in a puzzled way.

Thinking they might be lost, Tommy asked, 'Excuse me, can I help you?'

'We're here for the fair,' said the first. 'I'm Morris, and this is Norris, Horace and Boris.'

The other three men nodded at Tommy in turn.

'We're the morris dancers,' Morris explained. 'We're going to set up a maypole in the field.'

'Morris dancers?' Norris sounded surprised. 'I thought we were called norris dancers.'

'Norris dancers?' Morris scoffed. 'Don't be silly. Everyone knows morris dancers are called morris dancers.'

'I won't be doing *any* dancing if I can't get my bells fixed,' said Boris.

'What's wrong with your bells?' Tommy asked.

'He sat on them,' said Horace. 'And now they're all bent out of shape and he can't buckle them around his legs anymore. We're looking for a bell fixer.'

'I don't know any bell fixers,' said Tommy, 'but I'm the Keeper of the Blades from the castle, and I'm on my way to the

blacksmith's. I'm sure he'll be able to beat them back into shape. I'll take you there if you like.'

Tommy led the morris dancers through the town to the blacksmith's workshop.

'Easily fixed,' the blacksmith declared, and with three taps of his hammer Boris's bells were as good as new. 'And what can I  do for you today, Sword Girl?' he asked Tommy.

'Some tacks for Smith, please,' said Tommy.

She took the parcel of tacks and said goodbye to the dancers.

'Thank you, Sword Girl,' said Boris.

'You'll have to come watch us dance at the fair,' added Norris.

'I'll try,' Tommy promised, then skipped off to the cloth merchant.

Tommy was crossing the bridge over the moat on her way back to the castle when she heard someone calling her. Peering over the side of the bridge she saw Lil and the crocodiddle by the edge of the moat.

'Wait there!' Tommy cried. 'I've got something exciting to tell you!'

She ran down to the moat's edge. 'Sir Benedict has asked me to be in the tournament!'

'That's wonderful, Tommy,' said Lil. 'Well done.'

'And guess what?' Tommy continued.

'I'm going to learn to ride a horse, just like a squire!'

'Hmph. So now you've gone mad for horses too, have you? I suppose you'll be weaving ribbons in their tails next,' the crocodiddle muttered.

'Anyway, I'd better get back to the armoury,' Tommy said. 'Smith is waiting for these tacks.'

She hurried through the castle gate and across the courtyard to the armoury. 'Here you are, Smith. I'll see if Reynard needs any help with the swords.' She entered the sword chamber to see Reynard swishing a ruby-encrusted sword from side to side.

'What are you doing?' she gasped. 'That's Sir Walter's sword – you shouldn't be playing with that.'

'And what are you going to do about it?' Reynard demanded. But he put the sword back in the rack and said sulkily, 'Seeing as you're back, you can clean these swords yourself.' He gestured to the pile of swords that, if anything, looked bigger than it had when Tommy left for town. 'I'm going back to my own room.'

Shaking her head, Tommy sat down with her file and whetstone, picked up a sword and got to work. Not even sulky Reynard could spoil her mood. This time tomorrow, she'd be practising for the tournament!

CHAPTER 5

THE NEXT MORNING, Tommy hurried straight to the stables after breakfast. She passed through the archway that led from the great courtyard into the smaller courtyard outside the stables and entered the huge vaulted room that housed the castle's horses. The first thing she noticed was the noise: the cry of voices, the whinny of horses, the clatter of hooves striking flagstones. She saw some grooms brushing horses while others ran back and forth with saddles and stirrups as knights and squires shouted orders. Stable hands were mucking out the stalls – a very smelly job, Tommy realised as she drew closer.

'I'm looking for the stable master,' she said to one of the stable hands.

The boy pointed to a tall wiry man talking to a knight. 'There.'

Tommy stood to one side until the knight had departed, then stepped forward.

'Excuse me,' she said. 'Sir Benedict sent me. My name's Tommy, from the armoury. I'm here to learn to ride.'

'Ah yes, the sword girl.' He looked Tommy up and down. 'You're just a wee thing, aren't you? We'll have our work cut out for us getting you ready for the jousting in three days. Still, if that's what Sir Benedict wants … He told me to put you on old Bess. This way.' He jerked his head for Tommy to follow, but when they got to Bess's stall it was empty.

'Where's Bess got to?' the stable master asked a passing groom.

'Courtyard,' the groom called over his shoulder. 'I think one of the town lads was seeing to her.'

'Ah, so that's it. We're so busy because of the tournament we've had to get some lads in from town to help us,' the stable master explained.

He and Tommy walked out of the stables and into the courtyard, where a chestnut

mare was waiting, shifting uncomfortably from foot to foot.

'Here she is,' said the stable master. 'All saddled up for you already.'

'She's beautiful,' Tommy said, admiring the mare's long dark mane and glossy coat.

The stable master slapped the horse on the rump affectionately. 'She's a real lady is Bess. She won't give you any trouble. And mind you don't give her any trouble, either – Sir Benedict is powerful fond of Bess.'

Tommy approached the horse hesitantly. 'Hello, Bess,' she said, patting the horse on the neck. 'I'm Tommy. I've never ridden a horse before.'

The horse regarded her with deep brown eyes but said nothing.

'Now let's start at the beginning,' said the

stable master. 'You see this saddle we've got on here? That's your regular saddle, with a pommel to grip.' He pointed to a raised bit at the front of the saddle. 'For the jousting, you'll use a special saddle that's raised at the front *and* the back to hold you in place. There'll be no hanging on to the reins when you're jousting – you'll have a lance in one hand and a shield in the other.'

The stable master talked about saddles and stirrups, bridles and reins, till Tommy thought her head would burst from trying to cram in so much new information.

Half the morning had passed before he finally said, 'Right, let's get you on.' He cupped his hands and said, 'I'll give you a leg-up.'

Tommy swallowed. She'd never really

thought about how big horses were before but now, standing alongside Bess, she felt very small.

She placed one foot in the stable master's linked hands and managed to get the other foot into the stirrup dangling just below the horse's ribs. Taking hold of the pommel, she swung her leg over the top of the saddle.

'That's the way,' said the stable master.

But as Tommy came to rest in the saddle, Bess let out a shrill neigh and reared up.

Tommy screamed in fright as she rose high into the air and then was flung off the horse's back.

Ooph! Tommy hit the ground with a thud that knocked the wind out of her. Luckily she had landed in a pile of hay, which cushioned her fall.

'You all right there, Sword Girl?' the stable master asked, stretching out a hand to help Tommy up.

Tommy's legs were shaking as she got to her feet. 'I ... I think so,' she said.

She brushed the hay from her tunic while the stable master took hold of Bess's reins. 'There now,' he soothed, running his fingers through the horse's mane as she stamped and huffed. 'There now, old Bess.'

He turned to Tommy. 'I don't know what got into her. She's normally as gentle as a lamb. Come here, girl.' He beckoned Tommy closer. 'We'll give it another try.'

But as Tommy approached, the horse shied away, neighing.

'Bess,' the stable master scolded. 'Steady there.' He soothed the horse once more and Tommy again took a step forward.

The horse skittered sideways, snorting, her deep brown eyes rolling wildly.

'I never seen such a thing.' The stable master sounded mystified. 'Seems she's taken a real dislike to you, Sword Girl.'

A dislike to her? But why? Tommy looked at the horse in dismay; the horse appeared to be glaring at her.

'But what about my lesson?' Tommy asked. 'And the jousting practice?'

The stable master shook his head. 'There'll be no getting you on her back today, not with her all spooked the way she is. We'll just have to try again tomorrow.'

'But the tournament ... What if I'm not ready in time?'

The stable master shrugged. 'Sorry, Sword Girl. There's nothing I can do.'

CHAPTER 6

THAT AFTERNOON, Tommy joined the squires in the great courtyard for jousting practice.

When Sir Hugh entered, riding a large grey stallion, Tommy went up to him.

'I'm sorry, Sir Hugh,' she said. 'I don't have a horse today.'

Sir Hugh looked surprised. 'Sir Benedict told me you'd be on Bess.'

Tommy ducked her head. 'Bess ... doesn't like me,' she confessed.

'Doesn't like you?' Sir Hugh's forehead creased in puzzlement. Then he shook his head. 'We don't have time to find you a new mount now, Tommy. You'll have to practise on foot today. But mind you're on horseback for tomorrow's practice.'

'Yes, Sir Hugh,' Tommy murmured.

She went to the corner of the courtyard to fetch a lance and shield. As the squires mounted their horses, she could see them looking at her and whispering. Embarrassed, Tommy stared hard at her shield, which was painted with the Flamant Castle heraldry: a pink flamingo on a blue background. Her wooden lance, which was taller than her, was painted in pink and blue stripes.

The squires on horseback lined up and Tommy stood at the end of the line.

'Yesterday we practised charging,' Sir Hugh called. 'Today, we'll practise with the lance.'

Tommy concentrated hard as Sir Hugh demonstrated some movements with the

lance. She would have to use her lance to knock her opponent off his horse.

For the next hour, Tommy practised with the others as Sir Hugh rode up and down the line, watching and making comments.

'You handle the lance very well, Tommy,' he told her. 'But tomorrow we'll be practising jousting against each other, and you can't do that without a horse. So you and Bess had better learn to get along, understand?'

'Yes, Sir Hugh,' Tommy whispered, a miserable feeling welling in her chest. How could she make Bess like her? She didn't even know what she'd done to make the horse hate her!

When the lesson ended, Tommy returned her lance and shield to the corner and ran down to the moat, hoping to find Lil.

There was no sign of the cat, but the crocodiddle was backstroking lazily up and down the moat.

'Hello, Sword Girl,' he said, flipping over onto his stomach and swimming towards her. 'Why are you looking so glum? I thought you were excited about being in the tournament and riding horses?'

'I was,' Tommy said. 'But I had my first horse-riding lesson this morning and it didn't go very well.' She explained how Bess had thrown her off. 'I don't even know what I did to upset her,' Tommy finished.

'Maybe you were sitting wrong,' the crocodiddle suggested.

'But I don't know any other way to sit,' said Tommy.

'It's all about balance and grip,' said the crocodiddle knowledgeably. 'I could teach you.'

'You could?' said Tommy doubtfully.

'Of course! You don't need a horse – *I* can give you riding lessons. Come on, get on my back.'

Hopes rising, Tommy slipped off her shoes and pulled her leggings up to her knees.

'Ready?' said the crocodiddle when Tommy was sitting astride his back, her legs dangling in the weed-choked water. 'Here we go.' He began to paddle slowly into the centre of the moat.

'Oh!' Tommy wobbled wildly.

'Grip with your knees,' the crocodiddle told her.

Tommy squeezed her knees into the crocodiddle's side.

'Not too tight, your knees are digging into me. Relax a little. Grip firmly, but don't squeeze.'

Tommy was scared she would slide off if she loosened her grip, but she did as the crocodiddle said and found it was easier to balance if she wasn't squeezing so hard.

'That's the way,' the crocodiddle said. 'Now I'll go a bit faster.'

As the crocodiddle moved through the water, Tommy focused on the rhythm of his strokes and found that she was able to keep her balance quite well.

Faster and faster they went, circling the castle walls, the crocodiddle shouting advice. One lap, two ... After they'd

completed three laps of the castle, the
crocodiddle, breathing hard, swam over to
the bank.

'I don't think you've got anything to
worry about, Sword Girl,' he panted. 'You're
a natural.'

'Thank you, Mr Crocodiddle,' Tommy
said as she clambered onto the grass.
'You've really helped me. I'll be much
better on the horse tomorrow.'

'Horses,' she heard him muttering as she hurried back to the castle gate. 'So stuck-up. All they care about is having ribbons in their tails. They should use crocodiddles in tournaments. We're much more sensible.'

CHAPTER 7

Tommy went straight to the stables
the next morning, determined that today's
lesson would be a success. After her ride
on the crocodiddle the day before, and
everything she'd learned about balance and
grip, she felt confident that Bess wouldn't
throw her off again.

When the stable master caught sight of
her, he called, 'Wait there, Sword Girl, and

I'll have a groom fetch Bess from her stall.'

But Tommy could see the chestnut mare over by the hay where she had been the day before.

'She's already here,' Tommy called back.

'Is she?' The stable master sounded surprised. 'So she is. I can barely keep track of the goings-on around here.'

Together they walked over to the mare. She seemed to be regarding Tommy suspiciously.

'I've been practising my sitting,' Tommy told the stable master. 'I don't think we'll have any problems today.'

'Good,' said the stable master. 'Up we go then.'

He made a cradle with his hands and Tommy vaulted lightly onto the horse's back. But as soon as she put her weight on the saddle, Bess began to buck.

'Please,' Tommy gasped, clutching the pommel. It was no good. The horse bucked and twisted until she had dislodged Tommy, who fell heavily to the ground.

As the stable master helped her to her feet, Tommy blinked back tears of pain and disappointment.

'I've never seen Bess take against someone like this before,' the stable master said.

'Isn't there another horse I could ride?' Tommy begged. 'Sir Hugh said that I had to be riding a horse for the jousting practice today.'

The stable master shook his head. 'I'm sorry, Sword Girl, but we've no horses to spare.'

Before Tommy could respond, a stable hand ran up. 'Sir Walter is here, sir,' he said.

'Sorry, Sword Girl, I'll have to go see what his lordship wants.' The stable master hurried off after the boy.

'Why do you hate me so much?' Tommy asked the horse softly when they were alone.

Bess snorted. 'Because you're a cruel, vicious girl.'

'How can you say that?'

Tommy cried. 'What have I done?'

But the horse just stamped her hoof and turned away.

With a sinking feeling in her stomach, Tommy walked through the archway into the great courtyard. What should she do now? She couldn't practise jousting without a horse – and there was only one more day of practice left before the tournament! If only she knew why the horse disliked her so much ...

She would go back to the armoury and clean swords, she decided. At least that was something she was good at.

She trudged through the armoury to the door of the sword chamber. There she stopped, dismayed to see a dozen swords waiting to be cleaned.

Turning, she asked the smith, 'Where's Reynard?'

'You tell me,' Smith grumbled. 'That boy is never around when there's work to be done.'

Tommy entered the chamber, sat down and picked up a sword.

'We weren't expecting to see you back here, dearie,' said Nursie. 'We thought you'd be spending all your time practising for the tournament. Ooh, we are just so proud of you!'

'Thanks,' said Tommy dully.

'What's wrong, Sword Girl?' asked Jasper Swann, quick as always to pick up on her feelings.

Tommy threw her rag down in frustration. 'It's Bess,' she said. 'The horse.

She … she hates me!' Tommy had to fight to keep her voice from trembling. 'And I don't even know what I'm doing wrong.'

Bevan Brumm said wisely, 'Horses are mysterious creatures, Sword Girl.'

'Mysterious creatures, my foot,' said Nursie. 'Four legs and a tail – what's so mysterious about that?'

'What happened, Sword Girl?' Jasper asked.

'I don't know!' Tommy said. 'All I did was sit on her.' With tears in her eyes, she continued, 'I know I'll be letting Sir Benedict down, and you'll all be disappointed in me, but I don't have a choice: I'll have to drop out of the tournament.'

CHAPTER 8

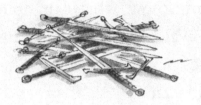

TOMMY WAS SITTING in the corner of the sword chamber, her knees pulled up to her chin, when Lil entered.

'What's wrong, Tommy?' the cat asked. 'I went to the courtyard to watch the jousting practice but you weren't there.'

'I won't be fighting in the tournament,' Tommy whispered over the lump in her throat.

'It's the horse,' Jasper explained.

'It doesn't like her,' added Nursie.

'Mysterious creatures, horses,' Bevan Brumm finished.

'I don't know what I'm doing wrong,' Tommy wailed to Lil. 'Every time I get on Bess, she bucks me off again. She called me cruel and vicious.'

Lil frowned. 'That doesn't sound right,' she said. 'I'm going to talk to her. Maybe I can convince her to give you one more chance.'

'There now, you see?' said Nursie comfortingly. 'All's not lost.'

'Indeed,' began Bevan Brumm. 'I think you'll find—'

But Bevan Brumm's speech was interrupted by a shout from the armoury.

'Sword Girl?' It was Smith. 'I've run out of those tacks again. Honestly, the way they're disappearing, it's like they've grown little legs and walked away. I need you to go into town to get some more.'

'Yes, Smith.'

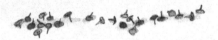

Tommy rushed through the streets of the town towards the blacksmith's, squeezing through the crowds of people.

'Look, it's the sword girl,' someone said.

Tommy turned to see the morris dancers, Morris, Norris, Horace and Boris, waving to her.

'Hi,' said Tommy, waving back, only to hear a sneering voice say, 'Hey, Sword Girl,

I heard your horse hates you so much you
won't be able to ride in the tournament
after all.'

Tommy spun around. It was Reynard.

'Maybe you'll have to ask Sir Benedict
if you can ride the crocodile instead,' he
went on. 'Ha ha! How stupid you'd look,
riding a crocodile in the tournament. Then

again, you always look stupid.' He ran away, laughing.

'Who is that nasty boy?' Boris asked.

'I know who he is,' said Horace. 'He's the one who tied the ribbons of our maypole in knots.'

'It took us hours to get them untangled!' said Norris.

'Ignore him, Sword Girl,' said Morris. 'The blacksmith told us you'll be jousting in the tournament. We'll be cheering for you.'

'Thanks,' said Tommy. She didn't have the heart to explain that Reynard was right, and that she probably wouldn't be in the tournament.

The next morning, Tommy was feeling too anxious to eat breakfast. Instead she went straight out to the courtyard to see if she could find Lil. The cat was waiting outside the kitchen door.

'Bess is going to let you ride her one more time,' Lil said. 'But she says that you're hurting her when you sit on her. I thought I'd come see for myself.'

With a sense of dread, Tommy followed Lil into the small courtyard outside the stables. Was she about to get thrown off the horse again? What if the problem wasn't just with Bess? What if all horses hated her? She kicked at a flagstone. If they did, not only would she have to drop out of the tournament, she'd *never* be able to become a squire ...

'What's he doing here?' Lil hissed.

Tommy looked up to see a familiar figure tie a chestnut horse to a railing then hurry away. 'Reynard!' she gasped.

When they reached Bess, Lil asked, 'What was Reynard doing here?'

'Reynard?' the horse asked. 'Oh, you mean the red-headed boy? He just puts on my saddle and leads me here from the stables. Then, after the girl has finished hurting me, he leads me back again. I think he must be one of the grooms from town.'

'That's no groom,' Tommy said. 'He's the Keeper of the Bows. What's he up to?'

'Take off the saddle,' Lil suggested.

Tommy unbuckled the saddle and, standing on the edge of a water trough, carefully lifted it from the horse's back. But she could see nothing wrong. Tommy was disappointed. She had been sure Reynard must be behind her problems with the horse, but it seemed not.

She patted the horse on the back, then quickly pulled her hand away. 'Ouch,' she cried, as the horse winced. 'What was that?' She looked closely at the chestnut coat and saw a number of small tacks embedded in the horse's hair. 'Tacks!' she exclaimed. 'Reynard must have been putting them under the saddle! That's what's been causing the pain, Bess. With my weight on the saddle they must have really dug into you. Hold still while I get them out ...'

'Why, that little sneak,' the horse said, outraged, when Tommy had removed the tacks from her coat. 'Why would he do such a thing?'

'He was angry because I was asked to fight in the tournament and he wasn't,' Tommy explained. 'I guess he thought if he could stop me from learning to ride, I'd have to drop out. And he was right, too. The tournament starts tomorrow and there's no way I'll be ready for it.'

'Oh yes you will,' said the horse. She sounded determined. 'Can you get into the saddle?'

'I think so,' said Tommy. From her position on the edge of the water trough, she put a foot into a stirrup. 'Yes!' she said, as she dropped into the saddle.

For the next hour, Bess taught Tommy how to walk and trot around the courtyard. When she was satisfied that Tommy had mastered trotting, she said, 'Let's go out into the field. It's time we had a proper gallop.'

A gallop! Tommy could hardly wait.

As they crossed the bridge over the moat, Tommy heard a voice call from below, 'Hey, Sword Girl, look at me! Look how fast I can go.'

Tommy glanced down to see the crocodiddle speeding through the water, arms and legs moving furiously.

'That's pretty fast, Mr Crocodiddle,' she called. 'But look at how fast *I* can go ... Come on, Bess – let's gallop!'

They set off across the fields, Tommy's heart thundering in time with the horse's

hooves, her hair streaming behind her. They galloped for miles, jumping fences and ditches, and Tommy never once lost her balance.

When at last they slowed and turned to head back to the castle, Tommy was laughing with pleasure. 'I've never had so much fun in my whole life,' she said.

'You're a natural,' Bess replied. 'I can't believe you've never ridden before.'

'I haven't,' said Tommy. But then she remembered the crocodiddle saying those same words: *You're a natural.* 'Actually,' she said, 'I have had a lesson.'

When they crossed the bridge again, Tommy urged Bess towards the edge. She wanted to thank the crocodiddle. But there was no sign of him.

'Mr Crocodiddle?' she called.

She thought she saw a ripple in the water, but when she looked closer there was no crocodiddle to be seen.

'I'll come see him later,' Tommy said. 'I don't want to be late for jousting practice!'

CHAPTER 9

TOOT-TAROOT!

As the trumpet sounded, Tommy felt a flutter of excitement in her stomach. She was sitting astride Bess, surrounded by squires on horses. She almost hadn't recognised the chestnut mare when she'd first seen her in a blue coat and hood embroidered with pink flamingos. Then again, Bess said she almost hadn't recognised Tommy in the new blue tunic and long pink cloak that Sir Benedict had surprised her with that morning.

The trumpeters began to move off through the archway leading to the castle gate. The procession of knights and squires followed, their cloaks billowing.

The road leading away from the castle was lined with townsfolk, all cheering the knights and squires. 'Flamant for victory!' they roared. 'FLAMANT FOR VICTORY!'

They were dressed in pink and blue and waved pink and blue streamers. Even the horses in the procession had pink and blue ribbons woven through their tails. With a pang, Tommy thought of the crocodiddle. She'd looked for him again the previous

evening but although she'd called and called, he hadn't appeared.

When they reached the field with the tents and platforms, the riders dismounted and stood by their horses. Tommy could see the knights and squires of Roses Castle at the opposite end of the field, the red roses of Sir Percy's crest bright on a white background.

Sir Walter the Bald and his wife inspected the line of Flamant Castle's knights and squires.

'Really, Walter,' Lady Beatrix the Bored yawned, 'this is so boring.'

'Now, now, dear,' said Sir Walter. 'Maybe you'd like to choose a knight to be your champion? That would make it more interesting, wouldn't it?'

'Perhaps,' said Lady Beatrix. She ran

her gaze over the knights. 'But the knights are all so boring.' She turned to regard the squires. 'And so are the squires ... Wait. Who's that?' She pointed her fan at Tommy, who felt her face grow hot.

'Why, that's our sword girl,' said Sir Walter, peering at Tommy. 'What's the sword girl doing there with the squires, Sir Benedict?'

Sir Benedict stepped forward. 'One of the squires was hurt during training,' he said. 'Since Tommy has proven herself to be skilled with a sword, I thought we'd test her skill in the jousting competition.'

'A girl in a jousting competition?' said Lady Beatrix, her eyes bright with interest. 'That's not boring at all!'

Then the trumpets sounded again and

Sir Walter and Lady Beatrix went to take up their seats on the viewing platform.

Sir Walter stood to announce the rules of the jousting competition that the youngest squires would be fighting in that afternoon.

'Each squire will be given three lances,' he declared. 'You will receive one point if you break a lance on the shield of your opponent, two points if you break the lance on his chest, and three points if you knock him off his horse. The match ends when one or other of the squires is unhorsed.'

As Tommy moved off with the others to the tents where the squires were to prepare for the jousting competition, her heart began to pound. How could she possibly succeed? Her opponent would have been training for weeks – even months – while she had only ridden a horse for the first time the day before!

'Come on, Tommy, I'll help you with your armour.' It was Sir Benedict.

'Yes, sir,' Tommy whispered.

He handed her a coat of padded cloth. 'Put this on first,' he instructed. 'It'll stop the armour from rubbing.'

When Tommy had slipped on the coat, Sir Benedict helped her pull a tunic made of chainmail over her head, followed by a breastplate, then he buckled armour onto her arms and legs.

Feeling uncomfortably stiff in the chainmail and steel plating, Tommy stood and watched as one by one the other squires went out to fight.

As her turn drew closer and closer, Tommy felt the flutter of nerves in her stomach grow stronger than ever. Why had she been so determined to fight in the tournament? she wondered. Now she would give anything not to have to go out there and fight with all those people watching her!

'The score is even,' said Sir Benedict as a squire from Flamant was knocked off his horse. 'We've won exactly half the bouts and the squires from Roses have won the other half. It's up to you to win it for us, Tommy,' the knight said, helping her onto the horse. He pulled her helmet down over her head, leaving the visor up, and gave her a lance and shield. 'Do your best and we'll all be proud of you.'

'Yes, Sir Benedict,' said Tommy, hoping

she sounded braver than she felt. Her pulse was racing so fast she thought she might faint.

As she rode out onto the field, Tommy could hear the crowd calling, 'Come on, Sword Girl!'

One voice rose above the rest.

'Sword Girl!' It was Lady Beatrix, and she was beckoning for Tommy to approach. 'Sword Girl, come over here.'

Nervous, Tommy moved Bess forward to stand in front of Lady Beatrix. What could the lady want with her?

Lady Beatrix turned to her lady-in-waiting. 'Eliza, help me get a ribbon out of my bodice.'

The lady-in-waiting unthreaded a ribbon and gave it to her mistress.

'Hold out your arm,' Lady Beatrix commanded.

When Tommy did, Lady Beatrix tied the ribbon around it. 'There,' she said. 'Sword Girl, you will be fighting for me today, so mind you do well.'

'Yes, my lady,' Tommy whispered, her mouth dry.

She cantered back to the starting position.

'Are you ready, Tommy?' Bess murmured as they lined up on one side of the barrier

that would separate the two horses. She was dancing from hoof to hoof, as if eager to begin.

Tommy drew a deep breath and pulled the visor down over her face. 'Yes,' she said. 'I'm ready.' She raised her voice. 'Flamant for victory!' she cried, and then she charged.

CHAPTER 10

THE TWO HORSES THUNDERED towards each other, the sound of their hooves muffled by the helmet encasing Tommy's head. From behind the visor, she fixed her eyes on her opponent's lance. It was aimed straight at her chest!

The spectators in the Flamant stands cheered when she managed to dodge the blow at the last second as the horses passed each other. Her own lance glanced harmlessly off her opponent's shield.

'Come on, Jem!' called the Roses crowd.

Tommy wheeled her horse around and, at the sound of the trumpet, charged once more.

She felt Bess's muscles rippling beneath her as she galloped, saw the bulk of Jem's powerful stallion streaking towards her, and felt a moment's fear at the clash to come.

As they met, Jem thrust his lance forward and struck Tommy's shield. His lance didn't break but the force of the blow was so great that she slid sideways in the saddle. Oh no! If she fell off she would lose the match! She struggled to right herself as Bess galloped on, but with a lance in one hand and a shield in the other she had no way to hang on.

Grip with your knees, she remembered the crocodiddle saying.

Tommy tightened her knees around Bess's girth and regained her balance. *Phew!*

They turned for the third charge and this time Tommy kept her knees tight around the horse.

'That's the way!' Bess cried as Tommy lunged forward with her lance, hitting her opponent's shield.

'One point for Sword Girl from Flamant!' Sir Walter declared as her lance snapped in two.

Dimly she heard the Flamant spectators hurrah.

Yes! She could do this! Tommy was no

longer nervous as she wheeled Bess around and accepted a second lance from a Flamant groom; she felt calm and focused.

The trumpet sounded and she charged. 'Flamant for victory!' she yelled as she advanced on her opponent. But suddenly she was reeling as her opponent's lance struck her chest. Over the clanging of the armour she heard the sound of a lance cracking.

'Two points for Roses!'

Tommy heard a disappointed groan from the Flamant stands and hung her head as she and Bess moved back into position. Now Jem was in the lead.

As the signal to charge rang out, she urged Bess into a gallop. 'Take that!' She drove her lance forward, aiming at her

opponent's chest. He leaned all the way back in his saddle, and the blow struck his shield. *Crack!*

'Another point for Sword Girl! That's two points each,' Sir Walter called from the stands.

Tommy cantered back to the starting point. Her breaths were coming in shallow gasps, sounding loud within the helmet. Bess, too, was heaving and snorting from the effort.

Sir Benedict was waiting with the groom. 'This is your last lance, Tommy,' he said.

'You've only got one more chance to strike a winning blow.'

'I can do it,' Tommy whispered to herself. 'I can do it.' She gritted her teeth, waited for the signal, and charged. 'As fast as you can, Bess!' she cried.

She reared away from Jem's lance while keeping her own lance centred on his chest. Her opponent teetered in his saddle and flung up his shield, the movement making him teeter even more.

'Victory for Flamant!' she heard the crowd cry as her lance bypassed his shield to hit his armoured chest with an almighty thud.

Her lance cracked and Jem tumbled from his horse and onto the grass.

The crowd erupted in cheers. 'Victory for Flamant! Victory for Sword Girl!'

Tommy raised her broken lance and shield above her head and whooped. Over on the viewing platform, Sir Walter and Lady Beatrix rose, applauding wildly.

'You should ride over and bow to Lady Beatrix,' Bess said, breathing hard.

Tommy cantered over to the viewing platform and bowed her head before Lady Beatrix.

'Well done, Sword Girl,' crowed Lady Beatrix. 'Come closer.'

Tommy urged Bess forward and Lady Beatrix pressed something into her hand. Tommy looked down. It was a purse full of coins!

Late in the afternoon, when the older squires had fought and an overall victory had been declared for Flamant Castle, Tommy left the others to their celebrating and headed off across the road to the fair.

As she neared Jonglers Field she saw the fair was in full swing. Jugglers and acrobats were entertaining the crowds – and there were the morris dancers, skipping around the maypole, holding long ribbons. When she drew closer, Tommy saw something that made her laugh aloud. They had used their ribbons to tie Reynard to the pole! He was shouting and struggling, but his shouts were impossible to hear over the music of the fiddlers. As pleasing as the sight was,

Tommy hurried on. There was something else she was looking for.

She reached the merchants' stalls and began to walk among them, clutching the purse Lady Beatrix had given her. The delicious smell of mince pies distracted her for a moment, but she moved past the pie stall without buying anything. There was a stall selling pots and pans, a stall for shoes and a stall for silks. Belts and buckles, combs and mirrors, pincushions ...

Ah, there it was. She hurried over to a stall draped with ribbons in every colour of the rainbow.

'Buying ribbons, Thomasina? I must say, I'm surprised. I never thought you were the kind of girl to like ribbons. Still, you deserve all the treats you want after your victory.'

It was the castle's cook, Mrs Moon.

'I should be in the kitchen preparing tonight's feast,' she confided, 'but I just had to come and see you fight in the tournament. We're all very proud of you, girl.'

'Thank you, Mrs Moon,' Tommy said. 'But the ribbons aren't for me. They're a gift for a friend.'

Tommy looked over all the ribbons on the stall before choosing the widest, shiniest pink and blue ribbons. She took some coins from her purse and paid for them, then hurried back to the castle.

With everyone still at the fair or celebrating Flamant Castle's victory on the field, the bridge over the moat was deserted.

'Mr Crocodiddle?' Tommy called.

There was no answer.

Tommy crossed the bridge and ran down the grassy bank to the moat. She couldn't see the crocodiddle anywhere but she was sure he was nearby.

'I fought in the tournament and won,' said Tommy shyly. 'I was so good at keeping my balance and gripping with my knees that the Roses squire couldn't knock me off the horse. But I couldn't have done it without you, Mr Crocodiddle. You taught me how to ride.'

A series of bubbles erupted on the surface of the water. Two beady eyes emerged from the murky depths, followed by a long snout.

'I bought you a thank-you present,' Tommy said.

'A present?' said the crocodiddle. 'For me? What is it?'

'Turn around and put your tail on the bank,' Tommy ordered. She held up the ribbons she had bought. 'They're in the Flamant Castle colours,' she told him.

'Ribbons for my tail,' the crocodiddle breathed, craning his head to look as Tommy tied them on. 'Thank you, Sword Girl. They're beautiful.' Tommy could have sworn the crocodiddle was blushing.

Tommy turned as she caught a movement behind her, and saw Sir Benedict, accompanied by Lil.

'Congratulations, Tommy,' said the cat. 'Sir Benedict says you fought extremely well.'

'Mrs Moon told me she saw you at
the ribbon stall,' said Sir Benedict. He
looked at the crocodiddle's tail. 'You're
a real champion, Tommy,' he said.
'And not just on a horse.'

'Hooray for Sword Girl!'
the crocodiddle cried, and
it was Tommy's turn to
blush as the others
joined in: 'Hooray!
Hooray! Hooray!'

join Tommy and
her friends for another
SWORD GIRL
adventure in

THE Siege
SCARE

CHAPTER 1

'GOODBYE! GOOD LUCK!'

Everyone at Flamant Castle had poured out of the castle gate to see off the knights.

Tommy waved until her arm hurt, then leaned against the railing of the bridge and watched till the knights were out of sight. Sir Walter the Bald, the nobleman who owned Flamant Castle, rode at the head of the procession. Sir Benedict, the

107

castle's bravest knight, was at his right hand. They were on their way east to Roses Castle. A month ago, Sir Percy and the knights of Roses had come to Flamant for a tournament. Now Sir Percy was holding a tournament at his castle, and nearly all the knights and squires of Flamant would be competing.

'I bet Sir Hugh is disappointed about being left behind,' Tommy said as the knight escorted Sir Walter's wife, Lady Beatrix the Bored, back inside the castle walls.

'Someone has to guard Flamant Castle and its lands,' Lil pointed out. 'But you're right. Nothing much will happen around here until the knights return – which suits me just fine.' The black and white cat stretched and yawned. 'There's been too much activity for my taste. I'm looking forward to a bit of peace and quiet and a warm patch of sun in the great courtyard.'

She began to pad across the bridge towards the castle gate and Tommy fell into step beside her.

'What about you, Tommy? The armoury will seem very quiet after all the hustle and bustle of getting the knights' swords ready for the tournament.'

'What I'd really like to do is spend some time looking after the Old Wrecks,' Tommy confided. 'I've been so busy with the other swords I feel like I've neglected them.'

'I'm sure they wouldn't agree,' said Lil. The Old Wrecks *had* been neglected for a long time, sitting dusty and unused in the darkest corner of the sword chamber. But when Tommy had become Keeper of the Blades she'd polished and sharpened them and found, to her astonishment, that the swords were inhabited by the spirits of their last owners.

For once the armoury was silent when Tommy entered. Smith had gone into town to see the blacksmith about some new shields, and there was no sign of lazy Reynard, the Keeper of the Bows.

Tommy went through the doorway to the left of the forge and into the sword chamber.

'Sir Walter and the knights have left for Roses,' she announced to the Old Wrecks.

'What a pity you couldn't go with them, dearie,' said a sabre from the rack in the corner.

Tommy, who had fought in the tournament at Flamant when one of the squires was injured, shrugged. 'I'm of more use here, Nursie,' she said as she pulled the sabre from the rack. 'After all, Sir Hugh and his men will still need their swords cared for.'

'Our sword girl has an admirable devotion to duty,' said the dignified voice of Bevan Brumm, a long-handled dagger.

'She does,' said the slender, slightly curved sword that was Jasper Swann. Jasper had been a squire, and was close to Tommy's own age when he'd fallen ill and died. 'But tell us again about how you won your jousting bout at the tournament, Sword Girl.'

So Tommy settled down with her file

and whetstone for sharpening, and a pot of clove-scented oil for polishing, and described her victory.

'Ooh, well done, Sword Girl,' said Nursie appreciatively. 'Of course, my little darling won every bout he entered ...'

Tommy thought she heard a groan from Bevan Brumm.

Nursie loved telling stories about her 'little darling', which was what she had called Sir Walter the Bald when he was a boy and she was his nursemaid.

'He had so much energy, you see,' she recalled fondly. 'He was always up to something. Oh, the mischief! One time he went missing for a whole day. My stars, I was in such a panic. I finally found him in the cellar. He said he'd been playing in an old tunnel. He told me it ran under the castle walls and underneath the town and came out in Skellibones Forest. Playing in dark, dirty tunnels was not at all what a young nobleman should be doing, I told him.'

'There's a tunnel running from here to the forest?' asked Tommy, interested.

'Oh no,' said Nursie. 'I'm sure he was just making up tales to fool his old Nursie.'

'There used to be rumours about a tunnel when I was a squire,' Jasper said. 'But no one ever seemed to know where it was.'

'I often wished for a tunnel when I was riding through the forest on dark, moonless nights,' Bevan Brumm said. He had been a merchant when he was alive, and had travelled widely. 'There's nothing worse than expecting a bandit to leap out from behind every tree.'

Tommy gulped. 'I hope *I* never have to travel through a forest on a dark, moonless night,' she said.

'If you ever do, you can take me with you, Sword Girl,' Jasper offered.

'Thanks, Jasper, I will,' said Tommy as a voice called, 'Hello? Is anyone here?'

Tommy ran to the door to see Sir Hugh pacing around the armoury.

'Hello, Sir Hugh. There's just me here, sir – Smith is in town. Can I help you?'

The knight held out his sword. 'Indeed you can, Tommy. I need my sword sharpened, and there'll be twenty more to be readied, too.'

'Twenty swords?' Tommy said in surprise.

Just when she'd thought things would be quiet in the sword chamber!

'That's right, and as fast as you can.' Sir Hugh's expression was grim. 'Yesterday Sir Benedict sent a couple of men out to patrol our western border and they've just returned with bad news. They spied a raiding party of a dozen of Sir Malcolm the Mean's knights from Malice Castle riding in our direction.'

Tommy put a hand to her mouth. 'Sir

Malcolm's knights are coming here?' she whispered.

'Sir Malcolm must have heard that Flamant's knights are away at the tournament at Roses,' Sir Hugh said. 'He obviously didn't reckon on the fact that some of us would be staying behind. But Sir Walter and Sir Benedict are smarter than that. I'm taking twenty men out to confront the raiding party. How soon can you have our swords ready?'

Within half an hour the armoury was as busy as it had ever been. Smith had returned from town to find Tommy hard at work. When she had explained why she suddenly had twenty swords to sharpen, the smith had immediately picked up a file and begun to help her. They worked side by side until finally, just as the sun was sinking beneath the battlements, they were ready.

Tommy could hear the stamping of hooves on the flagstones outside as Sir Hugh and his knights brought their horses round then hastened into the armoury to collect their swords.

After the last man had mounted his horse, Tommy and Smith followed them through the castle gate and onto the bridge. This time Tommy didn't wave cheerfully as she watched the small band of knights gallop towards the setting sun.

'Do you think they'll be able to fight off Sir Malcolm's raiding party, Smith?' she asked.

Smith let out a heavy sigh. 'Let's hope so, Sword Girl,' he said. 'Because if they don't, we've no one left to protect us.'

ABOUT THE AUTHOR

FRANCES WATTS was born in the medieval city of Lausanne, in Switzerland, and moved to Australia when she was three. After studying literature at university she began working as an editor. Her bestselling picture books include *Kisses for Daddy* and the 2008 Children's Book Council of Australia award-winner, *Parsley Rabbit's Book about Books* (both illustrated by David Legge). Frances is also the author of a series about two very unlikely superheroes, Extraordinary Ernie and Marvellous Maud, and the highly acclaimed children's fantasy/adventure series, the Gerander Trilogy.

Frances lives in Sydney's inner west, and divides her time between writing and editing. Her cat doesn't talk.

ABOUT THE ILLUSTRATOR

GREGORY ROGERS has always loved art and drawing so it's no surprise he became an illustrator. He was the first Australian to win the prestigious Kate Greenaway Medal. The first of his popular wordless picture book series, *The Boy, the Bear, the Baron, the Bard*, was selected as one of the Ten Best Illustrated Picture Books of 2004 by the *New York Times* and short-listed for the Children's Book Council of Australia Book of the Year Award in 2005. The third book, *The Hero of Little Street*, won the CBCA Picture Book of the Year in 2010. Gregory loves movies and music, and is a collector of books, antiques and anything odd and unusual.

He lives in Brisbane above a bookshop cafe with his cat Sybil.

THE *Terrible* TRICKSTER

'Tricksters are not welcome here.'

A trickster is turning life at Flamant Castle upside down. Someone has put sneezing powder in the knights' soup and itching powder in Sir Walter's sheets and changed the salt for sugar in Mrs Moon's kitchen. At first the tricks seem funny, but Sir Benedict is not amused. He thinks the trickster is Tommy – and unless the tricks stop, he will send her away from the castle! Can she find out who the real trickster is before she is banished forever?

Pigeon PROBLEMS

'The pigeon is missing!'

It's Lady Beatrix's birthday, and Sir Walter is planning a celebration at Flamant Castle. There will be games and competitions and a big surprise party. Everyone at the castle is excited ... except the pigeon. But the pigeon is needed for a very special job – and when he goes missing, it looks like Sir Walter's plans will be ruined. Can Tommy find her friend and save the celebrations?